DRACOPIS

dP

PRESS

Blue Swedish for Nowruz

Short Stories from Sweden

by Naeimeh Doostdar

& Azita Ghahreman

& Nasrin Madani

Translated from Farsi by Sholeh Wolpé

Dracopis Press

www.dracopis.com
beard@dracopis.com

Dracopis_005
Blue Swedish for Nowruz; Short Stories from Sweden
by Naeimeh Doostdar & Azita Ghahreman & Nasrin Madani

ISBN 978-91-87341-07-6
First edition. All rights reserved.

Naeimeh Doostdar & Azita Ghahreman & Nasrin Madani
are translated from Farsi by Sholeh Wolpé

The Karin Boye stanza on page 51, from the poem "I mörkret",
is translated from Swedish by Kristian Carlsson

Published by Dracopis Press, Sweden, 2015
EUROPE: Printed by Lightning Source, UK, 2015
USA: Printed by Lightning Source, USA, 2015
© 2015 Dracopis Press & the writers & translators

NAEIMEH DOOSTDAR (b. 1977) is a journalist and writer. She started working as a journalist during high school and has received several national honours in Iran. Doostdar also published poems and short stories, although much of her work has been nationally banned from publishing. In 2009 the political climate worsened in Iran and Doostdar was imprisoned because of her blog and other journalistic writings. Since 2012 she lives in Malmö, Sweden.

AZITA GHAHREMAN (b. 1962) is a poet and translator. She debuted as a poet in 1990 and published her four first highly acclaimed poetry collections before arriving in Sweden in 2006. Since then she has continued to publish poetry collections in both Persian and Swedish, and has recieved several international awards. She has translated Swedish poets like Tomas Tranströmer and Gunnar Ekelöf into Persian. She currently lives outside of Malmö, Sweden.

NASRIN MADANI (b. 1979) is a writer, critic and editor. She received her master's degree in Persian literature at the Azad University of Teheran, and at 18 she wrote her first novel. Although she has received numerous awards for her short stories, most of them have been nationally banned from publishing. She was forced into exile after being targeted by the Iranian authorities for her writings on women and minorities. She has been living in Sweden since 2012, nowadays in Malmö.

Naimeh Doostdar

The Notice

Each day, if they didn't pick up all the letters and news-papers, they wouldn't be able to open the door. Here, people still sent letters for every single thing: bank, insurance and taxes. Letters in a strange language that made no sense, a jumbled alphabet that added up to long words impossible to articulate in one breath.

The mail arrived at all hours. That first week a large packet was thrown at their door. When they rushed out to see what it was, they found a newspaper, much like their own hometown paper, Hamshahri, with all its daily ads, and devoid of news of any importance. They both rubbed their eyes and returned to bed.

It was easy to toss the newspapers in the bin specifically used for that purpose—fortunately, the Swedes cared about recycling—but they still had to open all the letters and read them carefully. When they had arrived in Sweden, someone had told them letters contained important information that if missed could lead to misfortune. Their destiny lay hidden somewhere in those letters.

They decided not to throw away anything that arrived in the mail, and they purposefully did not paste the "No unsolicited mail, please" sign on their door. Maryam believed it was possible there might be important information among the advertisement sheets, something like discount coupons for a big sale. She said they could even learn Swedish by reading the ads.

They read the letters with great difficulty. They typed them into Google Translate on their phones, word by word, and often got an awkward array of Persian words that made just enough sense to figure out, such as one from the local clinic, or another from a bank advertising its new credit card. But some letters were more important, like the ones that said when and where to take their child to the doctor.

When the gist of a letter sounded important, they'd take it to an old friend who spoke better Swedish, and he'd tell them where they needed to go or what they needed to do. Sometimes it took too long to reach their friend and the letter became outdated; sometimes it turned out the contents of the letter were of no importance.

Every morning, in the deafening silence of their apartment, they'd wake up to their own child's cries. The child was still confused by this country's daytime and nighttime hours. He'd wake up in the middle of the night and stare at the blackness beyond the window.

Maryam would get up and try to soothe him back to sleep. She'd take out her breast and put it in his 15-month-old mouth.

She had agreed with Ali to wean the child gradually, after they had settled in Sweden. Her mother had urged her to wait till the weather turned warmer—but when would that be? Ali said it wouldn't even begin to warm up till mid-spring, and even then, it would be ten degrees above freezing. That wasn't the kind of weather Maryam's mother had in mind. Her mother had also said they had to wean the child soon because it wasn't acceptable in this country for children this old to be breastfed. In the bus, people stared at her in amazement when she put him to her breast. Still, Maryam said, the child was just separated from her grandparents and if she took away her milk too, he'd be psychologically damaged.

In the dark, she'd stick her breast in his mouth and he'd fall asleep. And while he slept, that terrifying quietness would once again spread itself over their heads. Why were these people so noiseless? Why did nothing happen here? Why didn't the cars honk their horns?

One night, in the soundless darkness, Maryam heard the upstairs neighbors having sex. The child woke up and took some milk. She thought the noise was almost like moans, but it was the weekend and it wasn't hard to imagine that the people upstairs were having fun and screaming from pleasure. She looked over to see if Ali was awake but he was asleep, and the upstairs woman reached her orgasm. This was the only loud noise Maryam had heard since their arrival.

Maryam would stand by the kitchen door and watch a mother and father who sometimes brought their child to play in front of the complex. He was a quiet child who sat on a springy metal horse and quietly bounced up and down. The kids at the nearby preschool were the same way. A stone made more noise than those kids. When they first arrived in Sweden, her mother had called and asked what it was like over there. Maryam had responded, "Quiet. Very quiet."

One Monday morning, when Ali was at the university and the child was eating his breakfast, a stack of mail was dropped into the apartment. Maryam separated the newspapers and cut out a couple of McDonald's coupons, which she put into her wallet. There were three letters too. She sat at her computer to translate them.

The first letter was from the language school. It said in two weeks she could go to such-and-such an address to begin her Swedish class. The second letter was from an electric company advertising its electricity, purportedly cheaper than the one offered by the main plant. She typed in the third letter, word by word, then sentence by sentence, and still she could not understand what it said. So she typed the entire letter into Google Translate and tried to make a sense of the jumbled, broken Persian it delivered. She read it several times.

Your neighbor has contacted us and reported that she hears your child crying all the time and that he does not stop. It does not appear that your child is sick. She called us and reported that it seems the adults fight and they hit the child. To respond to this report, you must appear on Tuesday, 25th of February, at our address.

Birgit Jeppson / Jenny Nilsson

Maryam felt dizzy. She called Ali and asked him to come home immediately. Ali said he couldn't; he had just arrived at work and there was no reason to complicate things. Maryam burst into tears. She said, "You must come because this is urgent." She said she couldn't explain over the phone and that his work wasn't more important than her in this terrible state. He kept asking questions, and the child, who had been left alone in the other room, began to cry. Ali asked, "What is it that's so important it can't wait a few hours." Maryam lost her temper and threw the phone to the other side of the bed. The child was screaming and Maryam could at least manage to bring him to her bed and feed him. Her milk always calmed him down.

She had finally fallen asleep when she felt Ali's shadow over her. It was 2 pm and he had come home a couple of hours early.

—My professor didn't like that I left early.

Maryam picked up the letter from the table and laid it in front of him.

—What's this?

Confused, he stared at the incomprehensible words. The child was still asleep. Maryam showed him the page on Google Translate. Ali read it several times.

—What does this mean?

Maryam started to cry again.

—Maybe they're going to take our child away. Damn the day we stepped into this country.

Ali said she was talking nonsense. It wasn't easy to take people's children away. Maryam said this was Sweden, and they did things like that. She said that in this country if reports like this make it into the hands of the police, they'd take the child away. She said she read that on the website for immigrants to Sweden.

But what had they done? When did their child scream? When was he loud enough to make anyone think they were beating him? Ali said, "Let's think it through. Let's see what's happening. In fact, let's figure out where this letter came from? If it's from the police, why doesn't it bear the insignia and address of a police station? Which neighbor reported us?"

Maryam thought about the neighbors. She hadn't seen any. Once or twice she had seen a woman going off to do her laundry; the fat lady across the hall had the features of an Eastern European. Or, maybe it was the people upstairs who had reported them, the ones Maryam had heard moaning the other night. Who were they anyway? Maybe they'd heard the child cry the same way she had heard them having sex. Other than these, she had no memory of seeing any neighbors. It was as if no one lived in the building. The hallway was completely silent, and no one could be heard making any kind of noise. She had seen a stroller near the storage space but never heard a child running through the hallway or playing, never, not even once since they arrived five weeks and three days ago.

She looked out of the kitchen window. An old woman walked through the grassy space in front of the building, a carton of milk balanced on her walker. A few birds scavenged for food among the frozen blades of grass.

Maryam opened the apartment door and stepped into the hallway. She looked at her neighbor's door across the hall and read: Bruski. The one adjacent to their apartment read: Anders & Jonas Andersson. She ran upstairs and read the names on the apartment doors: Isabella, Ahmad, Mezgin. Mezgin was the one directly above them. They were the ones she had heard having sex. Or maybe it wasn't them. Maybe they had guests, and it was the guests she had heard having sex.

She ran downstairs. Ali had fallen asleep next to the child's bed. His hand was on the boy's little forehead. It was getting dark. Maryam looked at her watch; it was three thirty. Ali said, "Why did it happen this way?"

—What way?

—This way. What have we done? What does this

letter mean?

Maryam lay down. "It's the upstairs people. Sound travels through these walls. Or maybe it's the person next door, Anders. Have you ever seen him?"

Ali hadn't seen him. He said, "I've only seen an old man who comes downstairs to have a smoke. He doesn't look like any Anders, he looks more like an Arab. Besides, how do you know it's this Anders person?"

Maryam brushed her hand against the child's forehead. His hair was sweaty and wet. Ali said, "My innocent child. He never makes a peep. When did he ever scream?"

Maryam went over it in her head. "The night he ran into the living room door, remember? That night he cried for half an hour. His forehead swelled up. Or that time he wanted to watch cartoons on your tablet. You said no and took it away from him."

She remembered a lot more. The child was always crying. You could say anything and he'd cry. If you put food in front of him, he'd cry; if you took it away, he'd cry. If you turned off the light, he'd cry; if you turned it back on, he'd cry. In the bath... goodness... in the bath he cried nonstop; he screamed. He wouldn't let Maryam wash his hair and threw himself at the walls of the tub. The bathroom had vents. Perhaps that's how the sound traveled to the neighbors upstairs and downstairs.

—Do they think we torture our child?

Ali didn't answer. He got up and picked up the letter, turned the envelope over, read the address: Folkets Hus.

What was Folkets Hus? A social services office? Welfare agency? Maryam repeated the word she had seen in the letter: ANMÄLAN.

Ali came back to bed. "I don't feel like getting up. Do we have anything to eat?"

There was nothing. Maryam had been too preoccupied with the letter to prepare a meal. She realized she was hungry too.

The child whimpered and woke up. As soon as he saw his parents, he burst into tears. Maryam quickly put her hand on his mouth. Ali said, "What are you doing? Have you lost it?"

Maryam said, "But he's crying. They will hear him outside."

Ali took the child away from her. He hugged him and began to walk around, said, "Let him cry. We can't suffocate him. Fuck whoever complained about it."

Maryam started to cry. It was very dark. They had not yet turned on any lights. She pulled the blankets over herself. She could hear the television. Ali had put on the children's channel. The child quieted down and Ali came back to the bedroom.

Maryam thought it might be better to ignore the letter. As if it had never come. They could say they had never received it. Or that they couldn't understand what it said. She thought about returning to Iran.

Return and stay there. Ali could do whatever. He could stay and finish his studies, or return to Iran. To hell with his Ph.D., to hell with Sweden. From the very first day she hated this silent city. It was as if its people were all dead. The streets were void of car noises. No sounds of braking or honking. No bustle of human activity. In the mornings there were only the cries of the sea gulls and the sound of the postman throwing bundles of mail into the apartments.

Ali sat on the edge of the bed, said, "Do you remember the day we fought? It was dinnertime. You left the room and slammed the door behind you. The child cried. No matter how much I begged from behind the door, you wouldn't open it."

She remembered. But you couldn't call that a fight. She was only pouting. And only for two hours, at most. This fellow Anders, had he reported a door slamming? Didn't these Swedes ever argue? And if they did, did it mean each time the police, Folkets Hus or some other goddamn institution sent them a letter?

She said, "Don't you make it my fault. Have you forgotten you took the child to the park on Friday and he fell down? He was screaming when you brought him in through the hallway."

At that very moment the child came into their room, crying. Maryam thought, "Why is he so loud? Why isn't he like the other kids? What if there's something wrong with him? These Swedish kids never cry." Once she had seen a child fall from the swing. He didn't cry.

His mother didn't either. She brushed the dust off his knees and the kid went right back to playing. Now if he had been their child, he would have whined and screamed for a whole hour. What if they had spoiled their child? Or maybe the opposite, maybe they were too hard on him... maybe these Swedish parents simply said yes to whatever their kids demanded. Not like the Iranians who said do this and don't do that to everything. She had seen a child at the local library throw down all the books from a shelf and his mother didn't say a word. But in their home, it was always do this, don't do that.

Ali took a small box from a drawer and gave it to the child to quiet him down. Maryam asked, "Are we supposed to take the child too?"

Ali said, "Of course we do. We have to take him in, to show them there's nothing wrong with him. I'm going to give them hell. I'm going to demand they give me the name of the neighbor who made the complaint. I want to hear for myself what he was thinking. Maybe he thought since we're dark-haired, we're savages."

Maryam remembered a Kurdish woman at the library who had once told her the Swedes were racists. She had said, "You'll find out for yourself." She had said, "Don't be deceived by their smiles." Maryam had read on Facebook that the racist party in Sweden was gaining power and it wouldn't be too long before they kicked out all the immigrants. She worried what would happen to Ali if the university heard of the report.

Would they fire him? What if after four years, after he had completed his Ph.D., they refused him a job because of this? Just imagine, she herself had wanted to study Swedish and maybe even get a doctorate degree. But no, these people were way too racist. Ali was right. These neighbors had imagined Maryam and Ali were illiterates and didn't know how to treat a child. This Anders, or that woman Mezgin upstairs, or whoever reported them, was for sure a hundred percent racist.

Maryam said, "We have to gain the upper hand here. Who do they think they are? These racists make reports like this to say that immigrants are all this bad and therefore no good for society. They record these reports in their statistics and use them for the next election. I'm going to tell them I'm filing a complaint about them or about the neighbor."

Ali said, "Now hold on a bit, ok?" He admitted he had mentioned something about racism too, but maybe the real issue had nothing to do with that. Maybe it was a very responsible person who made the report. Someone genuinely worried about the child.

Maryam burst into tears again. "Do you mean someone kinder than me, his mother? What sort of a human being allows himself to put so much stress on a mother who's been in this country for just five weeks, turning her milk to poison? What sort of human kindness is that?"

Then she remembered she hadn't fed the child anything and went to boil a few eggs so they could all eat.

She said to herself, "It's good I didn't wean him so I can give him a little milk, otherwise he'd be upset and the police would come to the door and put us all in handcuffs."

After dinner, as Ali had taken the child to bed, Maryam went out to the hallway again. She held her breath to hear better. For the first time she could hear the television from the neighbor's place across the hall, the same lady she had seen take her clothes to the laundry.

* * *

Their appointment with Birgit Jeppson and Jenny Nilsson was at two in the afternoon. Ali had to get the time off from his professor. He wanted to tell him why, but Maryam had said no. She had said his professor was a Swede too and therefore probably also racist.

They wore their best clothes. Maryam combed the child's hair. Ali punched the address of the place into his GPS. It was a ten-minute walk from their building. They left a half hour early and arrived fifteen minutes before the appointment. The waiting room was empty. When they signed in, Maryam's heart was beating out of her chest. She imagined the receptionist knew the reason they were there. The child was in Maryam's arms, and he was wiggling to get down. Afraid that he might cry, she quickly put him down. When he took his shoes off and rolled on the floor, she said nothing. This is how the Swedes behaved, and no one ever said anything.

It wasn't clear where this was, a doctor's office or a social services agency. There were a few posters of men, women and children pinned to the walls. Maryam could only make out the word "family," the one that ended with "J" not "Y."

They waited ten minutes, then an old woman called them in. Her name was Birgit. She shook their hands and said Jenny was waiting inside. In the room, they all sat around a honey-colored table, on short-legged colorful chairs. In a corner of the room, there were a few toys. Jenny and Birgit stared at the child. Maryam let him down from her knees and gave him permission to go to the toys.

Birgit began to talk. She repeated everything in the letter, "A neighbor reported your child cries excessively, in an abnormal way that does not seem related to being sick." She also said, "This same neighbor has heard, several times, loud voices from your apartment... Do you acknowledge this?"

When Ali began to speak, introducing himself, explaining what he did in Sweden and where he was studying, Maryam tried to peek at the folder the woman was holding in order to see the name of the neighbor who had reported them. It was in Swedish, and all she could recognize among the words were ANMÄLAN, repeated three times in three sentences. Jenny took notes the whole time Birgit was talking, and they both kept a close eye on the child, who was spread out on the floor playing with the wooden toys from IKEA. It was one of those days when he didn't make a peep and was immersed in playing. Once, he threw a wooden box behind him. Jenny got up, picked it up and handed it back to him.

When Jenny returned to her seat, she stared at Maryam and said, "I will write a report on our meeting with you. Nothing specific will come of it. We will simply write our opinions. But if it happens again, this file will be re-opened for review."

Maryam stared into Jenny's eyes. They were not exactly one color but a sort of green that gravitated towards yellow. It was as if her pupils were frozen in one place; her gaze was dry and sharp.

Birgit asked if the child had any physical symptoms. Earache? Stomachache? Did he sleep through the night? She also asked about their relationship.

Maryam said the child was healthy and that he woke up once at night to breastfeed. Birgit said how wonderful it was that she was still breastfeeding, because mothers in Sweden did it for only six months and then returned to work. Maryam said she was a student in Iran and that she had just finished her studies. And that when she was a student she worked too. It had been only weeks since she'd arrived in Sweden and she had not yet been able to find a job. Jenny jotted down what she said in the file.

Ali told Birgit that he loved Maryam very much. This was the first time Maryam heard this from him in another language. It meant nothing to her. He said they argued very rarely and didn't have many disagreements, but that Maryam had not been happy since they had come to Sweden. Birgit asked why. Maryam said because it was too quiet. So quiet that sometimes she imagined she'd gone mad. She had become sensitive to even her own child's voice, and since they received the letter she took the child into the other room each time he cried, and closed the door. She said sometimes she went into the quiet of the hallway outside and listened.

Jenny did not write these things down. She put her green pen on the honey-colored table and went to the child. She picked him up and brought him to Birgit. The child burst into tears and began to struggle.

Maryam took the child and put him to her breast. He took it and calmed down. No one said anything. There was only the sound of the child sucking, fast and greedy. Maryam let out a loud sigh. Her tears fell on the child's small, round nose.

Azita
Ghahreman

Becoming Postmodern

When I was ten, my father read my diary and punished me. Later my boyfriend started reading it, looking for clues to my past love affairs. My husband sniffed it for signs of betrayal. My son, who was nine, read my journal and looked at me in surprise. My daughter read it to find out if I loved her more than her brother. Later, when I wanted to publish my book, the censor underlined some of the passages with a red pen and arched his eyebrows. I practiced writing in such a way so as not to get caught! I wrote and wrote and wrote and became so proficient at it that I learned a code for all the words and sentences, one that no one could break. Not even myself.

Please Come in

It's been three months since we moved to this building in the Sorgenfri district. We lived nine months on Davidshallsgatan and six months at some other place near Lönngatan. In our first place, only once did someone actually knock on our door and that, after four months of living there. I was delirious with happiness. This was such a rare occasion that I marked it as a major event. That beguiling sound of the bell while an actual person stood behind it! I opened the door to two old ladies, one in glasses, the other two meters tall, both from the church of I-don't-know-what. They had come to convert us. I made them promise to come again. I thought to myself, "Let them preach whatever they want. At least we'll have a cup of tea together." The second time someone knocked on our door, we were living on Davidshallsgatan. Knock, knock. It was ten in the morning. Excited, I ran my fingers through my hair and looked through the peep hole. Two schoolgirls stood there. I opened the door with a rookie smile and chatted with them in a mishmash of words I had learned at the Swedish language school. They had mistook us for Arabs and had questions about Arabic food and culture for a project at their school. I wanted to say, "Why don't you just come in! Is there a difference between what we eat, anyway?" But no matter how hard I thought about it, all I could think of were falafels. The third time someone knocked on our door seemed like ages later. He didn't ring the bell. It had been two months since we had moved to this building. It sounded like someone was scraping his nails on the door. It had been a long while since I had heard anyone at the door. My throat became dry and my heart started racing; by the time I convinced myself someone was actually there and moved myself to the door, the sound had stopped. I took a look in the mirror first. Maybe I was imagining things. I looked through the peephole—no one there! Whether out of consolation or just plain habit, I cracked open the door. There was no one there, just a newly created stinky pond, hot and vaporing. With great excitement, I took out my journal and wrote: "Today, 6th of November, something interesting happened. Around 9:20 AM, there was a knock on the door. I opened it. Our neighbor's new dog had left us a puddle of piss."

These Swedes

On our daily walk towards our car there was a large black plastic bag on the lawn, two meters away from us. It was tightly sealed. Judging from its bulk, it was quite full.

You said, "See? These Swedes are so cautious, indifferent, icy and cold that no one even bothers to throw a glance at this bag. They don't even care to know what's in it, or who it belongs to." I asked you, "Ok, so what's in the bag?" You said, "How should I know?"

And with that, we both sped past the bulky bag. A few days later, you asked, "What do you think is in that bag?" I shrugged my shoulders and picked up my steps. A week passed, then a month, and then autumn came. It rained every day, then came the snow, and each morning we walked as usual towards our car and returned home the same way. We'd glance at each other, then at the bulky black plastic bag peeking out of the snow, and shrugged our shoulders. We'd steal a quick look and pass it very fast, both of us silent but thinking of the same thing: These Swedes are truly strange people, indifferent, icy and cold.

The Golden Moose

At the Swedish language class, Ulrika always passed out handouts that began with a story, but this time the story's ending was mistakenly, and unbeknownst to us students, printed on a different page. Therefore each student felt compelled to come up with his or her own ending. The gist of the story was this: One fine spring morning the Andersson family woke up to find a golden moose with majestic antlers standing in their garden, chomping down their flowers and shrubs. Each of us now had to guess the rest of the story, putting ourselves in the shoes of this Andersson family. Ángela from Bolivia said if she were a member of the Andersson family, she'd call up all her friends and have a party so that they could all come and see the golden moose and dance some serious salsa. Hassan from Iraq said he'd put a rope around the moose's neck and tie it to the fence so that it couldn't stomp on the plants, then he'd call his kids to play with the creature while he went inside and asked his father what to do. Mina from Iran said, "I'd quickly get my camera and have everyone take a picture with him, then I'd send the pictures to Iran so that all our other family members could see." Jan from Bosnia said, "That's obvious; I'd hunt it with my gun." Nomo from Thailand just shook his head from left to right, and none of us knew what that meant. Shaun from Serbia said, "I'd look for someone to sell him to." Kemal from Turkey said, "I'd take the golden moose to the central square and let children ride it for a fast buck." Jameson from Congo said, "We'd quickly kill it, barbeque and eat it..." Our teacher, Ulrika, looked at us with wide, worried eyes and in a quiet voice said, "The ending to the story is on page five."

There, it read: The Andersson family quickly notified the police so that they could come and take the golden moose to the zoo.

Long Live Translation

My Portuguese friend, Regina, has read Khayyam's poems in French. She asks, "Why does America want to attack Iran?" I say, "For the same reason they attack other countries." Then, to make her happy, I say, "I've read Fernando Pessoa's poems and José Saramago's novels." She stares incomprehensively at me for a while, then it dawns on her who I'm talking about. She pronounces their names correctly. Then, surprised, she asks, "Do Iranians read such books? Is translation allowed?"

Badredin Harriri is a forty-seven-year-old Lebanese friend who has traveled twice around the world to reach here—from Beirut to Dar El-Salam to Zimbabwe to Stuttgart to Malmö... He takes out a ring that bears the Harriri family insignia and shows it to me. I hastily say, "I love Fairouz, Khalil Gibran and Nizar Qabbani." He raises his eyebrows and says, "Iran, Hezbollah, Shi'a..." then makes a machine-gun sound with his tongue. He leans over and quietly asks, "Is it true Iranian men take temporary wives?" He insists on seeing my eighteen-year-old daughter's picture. He looks at it and whistles, says, "Mamma mia!!" I have learned this is the best method to make friends. It seems that what connects human beings, soul to soul, is the world of the arts and politics. Sometimes naming a writer, singer or even a figure like Fidel Castro or Abdul Nasser forwards your relationship with someone by a few months. You figure out a great deal about their preferences, personality and thoughts, what they desire, who they are and their view of the world.

Nadia from Russia, Eva from the Czech Republic, Sofia from Poland, Simi from India, José from Argentina, Nini from Columbia, Ayami from Japan and Nicole from Mexico—my secret to making friends with all of them is mentioning Gogol, Kafka, Szymborska, Tagore, Borges, Paz, Márquez and Mishima... When they realize I know a writer or an artist from their country, at first they are delighted, then they ask where I'm from. Once I say Iran, they all ask the same things: Is it true Iranian women have to cover themselves from head to toe with a black piece of cloth, and that if anyone drinks alcohol he is whipped in public?

These days, I carry a picture of my daughter's birthday party in my bag. I have learned to show this picture instead of explaining how things really are. People look at it in disbelief; they say, "Is this in America?" They have only seen pictures of black-clad women, whips and so forth on television. They ask, "How is this possible?" It's difficult to explain how we Iranians have practiced for centuries to lead this kind of dual life. Jameson, my black friend from Congo, asks me to sit next to him for a picture. He speaks French better than his mother tongue, is in love with Édith Piaf, and everyone calls him Alain Delon, after the good-looking French actor. He wants to send our picture to his mother who is the principal of a school back home. He wants her to see what an Iranian woman looks like, that they don't all wear burkas, that they even attend universities and openly speak to men. I am reminded of the stereotypes of *Tintin in the Congo*.

Jameson says there are 700 different tribes in Congo, and they all fight each other. Jokingly I say, "Tell me, in your tribe, do they boil or barbecue human flesh?" He doesn't answer me; he picks up his camera and stomps off, bangs the classroom door behind him.

School for Mice

It's been three days since I began attending the school for mice. The school-building is an elaborate labyrinth in five stories, a Gustavian structure that connects to a few newer buildings through mysterious tunnels that curve and somehow merge into the same entrance and exit. They hand me a schedule that requires me to navigate these winding tunnels every two hours. Sociology in B:406, Swedish in F:123, English in M:209. I feel like a mouse in a maze looking for a piece of cheese, confused and hurriedly climbing stairs from one level to another. And then, when you get to room 209, out of breath, you realize that instead of M:209, you've arrived at N:209. You ask someone where M:209 is; they point to the basement. Now you have to go back four levels down, follow the signs to the right and to the left, then pass through several tunnels and senseless doors. You have to be aware not to go in a circle, passing the same signs, and to keep an eye out for a toilet too, because your bladder is about to burst. Just when you smell the cheese, a sign pops up right in front of your nose, informing you the corridor is under construction—and you run straight into a red brick wall! Now you have to backtrack, as if someone were toying with you and changing the location of the cheese. You get the feeling you are in a sitcom and every time you make a stupid mistake, they play a laugh track. That is, each time your nose hits a dead-end wall and you widen your eyes and pick up your tail to run, or you scratch your butt and look at your watch, it amuses an invisible audience watching you.

Right now, two goals: the toilet and room M:209. What can be funnier than a mouse running with a purpose and a full bladder, a heavy bag full of books, wearing high-heeled boots, coat and scarf? You either have to wet your pants or forgo the damn stinky cheese.

The Blind-City Project

How is it possible that they all behave the same every-where, whether in a bank or under a tree? Isn't all this seriousness strange? Imagine this, right now, in a bus: a middle-aged lady is about to board. She steps in. Her hair is wind-blown. She is sloppily dressed, wears a zippered red coat, and her umbrella has blue polka dots. After having slid her bus card she enters, and instantly tries very hard not to look into anyone's eyes. Not to bump into or brush against anybody. Not to sit next to anyone. And then, through the long journey, she stares out as if gazing at some hidden, distant star through an invisible telescope. Passive, staring with-out any enthusiasm, without moving her head to the left or to the right and, most importantly, without ever smiling. The next person. A young man in a red rain-coat. Music in his ears. His pants slipping off his butt. Sure! He moves along just like the other one, until he finds the farthest seat at the greatest distance from everybody and plunges himself into it. The third person climbs in at the Jägersro bus stop. She is a young lady with a stroller. Just like the other ones. Except she goes and stands next to a window and the whole time stares out, except for occasional glances at her own baby.

Ok, so I decided to do something radical. I started my project in the beginning of the summer. I wanted to give the Swedes a dose of my experiments in good weather. However, I ended up beginning the project on a cloudy day. First, I smiled at whomever I passed in the streets. Very simple, without guile or embarrassment. If the person wasn't paying attention or resisted, I'd attract his or her attention with a horrendous cough or a sudden stumble-like movement, until he or she noticed me. Out of the ninety-six people I smiled at during these five days in Malmö, only four old ladies returned my smile. Two of them even said a few words under their breaths, which I took to be complementary. Seven middle-aged women muttered something angry, which is worse than cursing, though three of them made suspicious faces that was hard to interpret. The men were the worst; they did not react at all, except for four, the first of which, wheelchair-bound and bored, was people-watching. The next two just stared at me. As if the sky had fallen. The last one, who had a lot of stuff spread out around him and probably was a Bosnian, invited me to check out his merchandise.

My smile angered young women, especially if they

were alone. The best group in my experiment was babies in their strollers. They were fantastic. They would turn their heads to look at me again. They'd wave and laugh, so much so that their mothers were compelled to notice me as well. I wasn't satisfied with my results. This scheme wasn't good enough for the Swedes.

The week after, I began my touching test, which was more complicated; it included rubbing shoulders, suddenly running towards someone walking in my direction, forcing my way between two people walking side by side and, most importantly, smiling and looking into their eyes while doing it all. Out of seventy experiments in the course of four days, fifty-seven were of interest. Twelve walked by without ever changing their demeanor. As if I were a mosquito, or the sound of a fart. Ten people emitted a frightful noise. Three pressed themselves against the wall in anger or surprise. A few raised their hands to defend themselves. The rest said things I didn't understand, but all in all I was satisfied. The Swedes could indeed show reaction. Then how come they walked through the streets as if they were stiff mannequins marching on ice?!

The following month I merged my methods. I combined smiling and brushing against someone while coughing loudly, running towards someone and peaking at the newspaper he was reading as if I were interested in it, or screaming in someone's ear as if I had just seen a polar bear in the middle of the café. Stepping on people's feet while at a bus stop, a movie line, or restaurant produced the most interesting results. Without exception, it evoked cries of pain from everybody. It all became difficult, oppressive work. I had heard that scientific discoveries always pass through difficult, complicated roads. I read this in Discovery Magazine about Newton and Einstein. Attention to my observations was wavering. I had come to situations that were contradictory. I got confused about the accurate calculations for reactions. But in the end I was able to find a grand new method that combined it all: grabbing purses.

I was only two days into practicing my new experiment. I'd quickly grab a person's bag, then after the victim started screaming, I'd say, "Smile! You're on Candid Camera!" I'd then return the purse and quickly give him or her a hug. It didn't take long before I was arrested at a self-service restaurant for retired cops. At first they asked, "Where is the camera?" Finally, after many questions, answers and explanations, they figured out I was not a thief. After having told them about my experiments, I was put on an involuntary cocktail of pills. They sent a social worker to my home and made me go to group therapy where I had to confess to all the dirty stuff I had committed when I was much younger. Well, as they say, one must walk the city of the blind with one eye closed. Now I have become like everyone else. Have you ever looked at those big green buses with fogged-up windows? All those faces blankly staring outside? I am one of them. That person in the ugly black coat, holding onto the metal railing and silently staring at something distant, something unknown, out there.

Nasrin
Madani

Occupied Land

Jag är bland dem som knappast finns
och bara vet och bara minns
det gamla mörkrets hjärteslag,
som väntar ingen morgondag.

som fruktar ingen morgondag.

Karin Boye

Like those who barely live at all
I'll only know and do recall
old darkness' pounding sorrows,
waiting for no tomorrows

fearless of no tomorrows.

Karin Boye

Maria divides the bread between us. I wipe the mildew off and close my eyes as I break it into pieces in my mouth. It is possible this is the last piece of bread I'll ever eat before a bullet hits my head from behind and blows it up like a watermelon, sending blood and brain tissue flying out onto the walls and that painting of a naked woman with arched waist and white curvaceous buttocks.

We satisfy our thirst with snow, the kind of snow that is a bit cleaner than the one smeared with blood and dirt. There are bodies everywhere. Bullet-ridden bodies and execution fields have fucked the lungs of northern Europe and the delicate freshness of this green land.

We've been wandering around for days, moving from one ruined building to another. To where? Maria throws a pebble at me from across this room that once might have been a sitting room and probably has seen its share of parties and laughter. She gestures shut up.

The Russian patrol could pop out of anywhere to eliminate us.

There are no bells to toll for the death of so many; no priests to bless them, no relatives and friends to shed tears on their blown up, burned or disintegrated bodies.

My heart has become accustomed to the frightful sound of the bombs. Last night I had another nightmare about that damned deer. That deer, and that woman.

It was dusty and smoky. Åsa and I were hiding behind some fallen fir trees. We were near a few cabins. A Russian officer came out of one cabin, and a few soldiers dragged a deer out of a barn. They had tied a rope to the antlers. The deer's left knee was broken and pieces of its skin were torn up. The deer was letting a heartrending cry out of its throat. The officer went to the deer and drew a knife from his belt. As he walked towards it he rubbed the tip of the knife on one of his fingernails. When he reached the animal, he bent on his knees and with one blow plunged his knife in the stomach, then lifted his own head, opened his other arm to the sky, and let out such a thundering, frightful howl that the cries of the deer disappeared inside it. He was up to his elbow in the deer's stomach; the animal's innards hung out and the blood flooded the ground. The deer fell on its side and a gurgling sound bubbled out of its throat for a while until it gradually subsided. The officer wiped the blade of his bloody knife on his own uniform. A soldier holding a child's dress ran to him and began to wipe away the officer's hands and bloody sleeve with it. Another soldier ran out of another cabin with a wooden chair, so the officer could sit down and catch his breath. The officer then nodded to a soldier and from a cabin near us the soldier brought out a young woman. She had long blonde braided hair and wore a thin white dress revealing the firm curves of her body and thighs. Her dress was bloodstained. One of the soldiers kicked the back of her legs with his black boots and she fell to her knees in front of the officer.

The officer stroked the woman's hair. Disdainfully, she pulled her head away from under his wide hands. The officer let out a sinister laugh and pulled out the knife from his belt and began to stroke one of his own fingernails with its blade. I feel a distant pain that is always getting closer; I feel it in my ribs. I want to swallow my breath, but I can't. It's like they are sitting on my chest and have their hands around my throat. My eyelids are heavy. Something sparks in my eyes and I open them to find Lars has put his hand over my mouth. Maria pokes my ribs with her gun, tells me, "Shut up! The Russians are too close." We stay still for a few seconds, then Lars removes his hand from my mouth and I take a deep breath.

That pose and look from years ago remains as vivid as this half-burned painting in front of me, so alive and shiny on the timber wall of this bedroom with its broken wooden bed and crushed chair from IKEA. Two balloons and three people, one of them a child with open arms and a yellow balloon, the second one with open arms and a red balloon, and the third one with half of her body burned, and an inscription that reads: "Birgitta's drawing at age four, March 2025."

In Aftonbladet, Putin stood in a rectangular cadre, and wore a black suit with a tie the color of which I don't remember. In that picture, the soldiers standing in the cadre were giving him military salutes. Putin's hands betrayed more of his character than his Siberian face and those two obstinate decisive blue points in his head. His fisted iron hands were as hard and impenetrable as the Russian-built war tanks exported to third world countries, hands that signed the eternally hateful nuclear agreements uniting with the hellish barbarian to kill, destroy and bomb all civilizations, so that this drawing of people with balloons can hang half-burned, and for misery to become the share of the people, the animals and this forest. Those hands bore remnants of the frightful Gulag. Those same hands, years ago designed the plan to dispatch submarines to this land that now lies wasted and burned.

From the black and blue hollows of his eyes, he had traced a track of blood through Stockholm. The Old Town with its cobblestone streets in bright nights, the Dramaten theater with its paintings and statues, the Royal Castle and its antiquities, the Public Library and its philosophy books, Stortorget and its night clubs and bars—all lay in majestic humiliation; and the dust of the graves of all the churchyard's dead were sprinkled by those same hands on the cities and forests of this large burial ground. The earth committed suicide from those years in order to arm itself.

Lars in a low voice asks me how many may still be alive; with his index finger he traces a circle in the air. With my index finger I draw a box, and whisper, "As long as the atomic bomb..." suddenly frightful barks of a dog alert our hands and eyes. We look out through a slit in the wall. A terrified dog with a lame leg, trailing blood, moves his head to and fro, and settles down by the back wheel of a broken bicycle. His tongue, hanging out of his mouth, moves with his every burning breath. We can see three loudmouth Russian patrolmen behind one of the destroyed homes. I place my finger on the trigger and prepare to shoot. Lars who has taken the corner parallel to me, wipes the sweat off his forehead.

The patrolmen walk in short strides towards the dog. The dog jumps, and barks in staccatos. Limping, it runs and wanders through the ruins and approaches our hiding place. I throw a glance at Lars. He pulls his head away from the slit in the wall, holds his breath, and places the gun on the floor as lightly as the dancing feet of Maya Mikhaylovna Plisetskaya. He then puts his head between his knees.

I aim at one of the hat-wearing Russian patrolmen. The dog gets closer, but the hubbub of a dozen or so Russians dissuade me from shooting. I lose my breath for a few seconds, swallow hard, and murmur, "Don't come here. Go away. Go." I try to will the dog away from our hiding place. We can hear it downstairs, near the front entry. Suddenly, gunfire breaks the anxious silence of my mind and after a few seconds of quiet, there are guffaws and the sound of guns firing into the air.

The patrolmen start a bonfire in the square near the children's playground with its shattered slide and cut up swings. They dance and drink and throw bottles hither and thither. They pull down each other's pants and fuck one another; they throw the dog's body into the bonfire. After a few minutes the stench of the animal's charring body fills the air.

I want to go somewhere far away where I can run around naked, without guns or backpack. Lars has crumpled into himself and has fallen asleep with his hands over his ears.

We are scattered in different tiny groups. Lifeless corpses of the tender-aged Russian soldiers are visible amongst the remains of animals and other humans. Their bodies are torn into pieces and bullets have made their eyes explode; but who will ever find these atrocities significant at all? Who will care? When we accidentally encounter one another in the forest or in half-burned cabins, in ruins of apartments or in empty mortar-shelled roads, we hear so many tales of cold-blooded murder that all of the stories in our heads sink us into a dark sedated sleep.

Ismael and Karl have put down their guns. We have a small party and give Karl a piece of bread in observance of our tradition. Karl, with his blonde beard and excited eyes in which youth's wonder blaze, shows the bread to Ismael in amazement.

The last time we saw Ismael he had spoken of a party with plenty of food, boys and girls, hashish, wine and cigarettes. That was a long time ago.

The four of us sit in a circle on the floor and exchange felicitations by silently moving our lips. But, happy what?

It's been days since Maria disappeared, and Lars still does not know that I saw her through the slit in the wall; her body hung from a tree, naked from the waist down, her thighs bruised and full of knife cuts.

Maria knew she had to do something about Åsa's nightly nightmares, her unpredictable screams. The Russian patrols were everywhere. Åsa, after she saw the butchering of the woman in a white dress, could no longer keep her nightly nightmares and madness at bay. It was for this reason Maria suffocated her.

Lars sticks a twig in the ground between us, puts his hand in his coat pocket and we all make believe he has pulled out a lighter. He holds the make-believe lighter over the twig and snaps. The twig lights up. We believe to gather around a fire.

What now has connected a "Sverigedemokrat" to a "Socialdemokrat" is this very earth bruised and swollen beneath the Russians' boots; this very dying land.

Their disagreements, hatred and threats have all become smoke in this dead-end darkness. Karl, in a state of ecstasy, sings a song by silently moving his lips. He puts the bread in his mouth and sucks on it, then gives it to Ismael who does the same. Then it's my turn. After I have sucked on the bread, Karl wants to eat it. We watch him as he puts the softened bread in his mouth, our own mouths half open. How old is Karl? Sixteen? Eighteen? Twenty?

Our blissful break from our fear of the patrols is over and we each crawl back to a corner, but Karl still basks in a halo of happiness and a new life.

Fresh mass graves, pieces of rabbit bones, birds whose wings have been pulled off, the dogs and this cloudy sky, all transport me to a distant past; a time of healthy springs, passersby holding ice cream cones, people with dogs, bicyclists, men and women pushing strollers, people running or exercising around lakes; days that have now been diminished to sad, expired memories by the gloom and tragic deaths of these times.

A male bird is trying to mount a female bird. Without missing a beat I aim my gun at one of them, but suddenly remember that the patrolling soldiers are everywhere.

The male bird's struggle to mount the female expands in my mind. A mild ache shoots across under my left breast. I throw the gun's strap on my shoulder and squeeze my breasts. Escape? Escape? Escape? To where? Wouldn't we fall into another trap in that disappointing seclusion? Lars has found something; he bends over and puts it in his mouth. I run and stand in front him. He is chewing something. I put my hand on his jaw and try to force his mouth open. I put my mouth on his. His lips and teeth open. With my tongue I pull out a portion of what's in his mouth and begin to chew. I put my tongue in his mouth again. He locks his teeth and traps my tongue. I see a barbaric mauling ferocity in his eyes. If he squeezes a little more... just a little... he eases the pressure of his teeth. I pull out my tongue. He pushes me down. I lean against the trunk of a tree. He comes towards me, panting. He puts his hands on my breasts and squeezes so hard I involuntarily let out a cry, and startle a few birds out of the branches. He unhooks his belt; I help him do it with maddening speed. My gun falls from my shoulder. He bites my neck so hard that a burning pain lodges itself under my skin. I pull down his pants. His knees shiver. I bend, bring my head down... unfamiliar, commanding words carrying a Siberian chill freeze my body. A gun's barrel points to the back of Lars's head. Lars, shocked and surprised, gives in with his body. A Russian coat comes out from behind a tree. I lift my head up and the sight of a knife's sharp edge rubbing against a fingernail fills my eyes. Lars is like a fly trapped in a spider web. The Russian soldier takes Lars's gun away and commands him to take off his pants; at the same time he kicks my gun into the bushes, far from me. I force the smell of those devils into my lungs. The officer comes towards me. He puts a hand on my shoulder to help me up. My head reaches to the level of his shoulder. He moves his knife towards my left breast. My breath locks in my lungs. Devilish mischief has nested in his eyes. He slides the edge of the knife over my face. I feel a burning wetness on my cheek. The pale unmoving blue of his eyes wants the death of a living thing. The Russian soldier aims his gun at Lars and from time to time looks over at the officer and lets out a guffaw at every one of his moves. The officer pushes my shoulder down and forces me to bend over. He pulls aside the front of his coat and wants me to open his belt. His breathing has altered. I undo his belt and lower my head. The soldier jumps up and down like a lunatic. Lars has his hands locked behind his neck. He and I exchange quick glances. The officer pulls my head towards his stomach and says something in Russian. I pretend I'm going to do as he asks and say, "Ja, ja," but quickly pull out a knife from behind my belt and land it on his fingers. It cuts deep through. The officer screams. The soldier, confused, pauses and turns to look at the officer. Lars, without losing a second, turns the gun's barrel towards the soldier and pulls the trigger. I run with all my might, sending back quick glances. I see the officer has taken out his handgun. I keep my head down and run zigzag. I run. Run, and in the tumult of Russian words, recognize Lars's voice moving in another direction yelling, "Another one went to hell."

The smell of gunpowder and the stench of rotting corpses make breathing hard. Through the slit in the wall the sun's pale glow falls on my right hand. I throw a pebble at Lars. He notices the light and my hand. I rotate my hand and move my fingers as if I'm holding a glass of wine. I release my hand in the empty air and let the faint light shine on my wrist and fingers. Hand and light dance together. Lars shakes his head, smiles, and sings a song under his breath. I try to coordinate my hand movements with his lips. I begin to move my head too, and in this distance from one another we smile at each other. Noise of familiar and unfamiliar language enters through the wall. It comes from the soccer field across from us, its grass torn up by mortar shells. I put one eye over the slit in the wall. A group of Russians have encircled Ismael and Karl. They have stripped them naked and are now forcing them to run. From here it looks like Ismael's legs are injured, and Karl is holding a bloodied arm against his body. He tries to go back and help Ismael but can't because of the gun shots at his heels. Ismael falls down. A soldier goes to him, lifts him backwards by the neck and pulls out a knife. A few seconds pass before Karl looks back. When he sees Ismael's dead body, he lets out a heart-rending cry and falls to his knees.

They play soccer on the torn up field, shooting bloody balls towards the goals of lunacy. Lars crumbles into himself and lays down on the ground.

These raw, rotten potatoes are as delicious as the bar-
bequed sausages of distant summer evenings. A feeble
light breaks through the grey clouds. Lars has held
his face up towards the light; his eyes are closed. I say
his name: "Lars." He opens his eyes. I go to him. The
essence of his body heat has accumulated in his blue
eyes. Something inside me flaps its wings and prepares
for flight. I take his hands and put them on my breasts.
He smiles. I unbutton his shirt. His white, hairy, sweaty
body arouses me. I put his hand on my cheek. I breathe
in his tangled hair. The odors of dirt and gunpowder
are intertwined with the droplets of sweat on his forehead. We lay side by side on the ground.

A portion of the roof has caved in. We take off our
clothes. I hide my handgun under the pile of clothes.
We stare at one another's naked body in fiery silence.
We smell each other's hair and every other part of each
other's body. He kisses and licks the space between my
fingers, my underarms, and under my breasts. How
long has it been since a hand touched our bodies
in kindness and love? Since someone planted a kiss
on our lips? I kiss him and softly bite the side of his
mouth, and as I watch his lips blush, my desire to bite
them surges even more. With tongue and teeth Lars
plays with my nipples. His fingers and palms press
firmly and pleasantly on my hips. He pulls me tight
against his stinky body, not leaving an inch between
us. I wrap my legs around his. He sucks on my neck. I
feel a painful, life-giving pressure from his hard penis

in my vagina, and with each hump, he kisses my lips and plunges his tongue into my mouth. Our laughter entwines from pleasure and bliss, from sighs and pain. We pull into ourselves all blood and injuries, all death and life, and in this way the smell of our sweat and hungry bodies prevail over the smell of gunpowder and clotted blood. From one pain we crawl into another pain. We bite each other and pull one another's hair and in this way break the spell of gloom's desolation and boredom. There is an incoherent distant sound, but we don't want to stop. My legs are spread open and hang on each side of his body. He licks the sweat off my face and his endless blue eyes spread themselves on the expanse of my eyes. He kisses my earlobes with his red lips and whispers, "It's finished. They are above us. We're done."

I slowly reach towards my clothes. I feel the hardness of my gun. I turn quickly towards the ceiling. The Russian soldiers, the howling of hyenas, a bandaged hand over a coat, and a knife in the other hand. I close my eyes and wish to take revenge on this damned life with my pleasure. We wrestle. We wrap around each other; our bodies become like a knot in an executioner's rope. I twist my body one last time. Lars says, "They are coming." I press my breasts on his hairy chest. I am counting my breaths. I press my lips on his lips, and bite the side of his mouth. He lets out a pleasure-filled cry. I take my gun and put it on his temple. His eyes rest on mine for a moment. Surer than death, he closes his eyes and slowly opens them again. A satisfied smile spreads on the side of his lip, and he then closes his eyes. I pull the trigger.

Lars's blood and pieces of his brain splash across my face and neck. I lick the blood from the side of his lip. I lock my body on his, like a lover's rendezvous on a bridge. I close my eyes and for a moment see the butchered woman in white passing through. The officer reaches the door. He howls "Het" with his angry black and blue satanic eyes. I smile and pull the trigger.

SHOLEH WOLPÉ (b. 1962) is a poet and literary translator. A recipient of the 2014 PEN/Heim grant, 2013 Midwest Book Award and 2010 Lois Roth Persian Translation prize. Wolpé is the author of three collections of poetry and three books of translations, and is the editor of three anthologies. She lives in California, USA.

CPSIA information can be obtained
at www.ICGtesting.com
Printed in the USA
FSOW01n2051220615
8176FS